D0460883

For More Information Contact:

Downtown Wetmore Press

13451 Wetmore Road

San Antonio, Texas 78247

ISBN 978-0-9795302-0-3

Library of Congress Control Number: 2007903166

Text Copyright © 2007 by Miriam Aronson and Jeff Aronson

Illustration Copyright © 2007 by Downtown Wetmore Press

This book is a work of fiction. Names, characters, places, and incidents are either products of the authors' imaginations, or are used fictitiously. Any resemblance to actual events or locales or persons, either living or dead, is entirely coincidental.

All rights reserved. No portion of this book, except for brief review, may be reproduced, stored in a retrieval system, or transmitted in any form or by any means - electronic, mechanical, photocopying, recording, or otherwise - without written permission of the publisher.

If you would like additional copies of *Little Mike and Maddie's First Motorcycle Ride*, please visit:

www.CrumbGobblerPress.com

Little Mike and Maddie's First Motorcycle Ride

Miriam Aronson
& Jeff Aronson

Illustrated By
Jay Zephyr
& Jeff Aronson

Little Mike and Maddie were very happy and had all the things two dogs could ever need. They lived in a nice house with Big Bob and Amy, who gave them lots of love. Their backyard was filled with toys, and their bowl was always piled high with yummy treats.

Everybody liked Little Mike. He was Maddie's best buddy, but
sometimes he was a rascal. He loved to run off with her ball just
so she'd chase him. Maddie was the sweetest of dogs and everybody
liked her, too. She loved to eat, take naps, and play with Little Mike.

The weekends were especially fun when Little Mike, Maddie, Big Bob and Amy were all home together eating their favorite breakfast of pancakes and bacon...

and playing ball in the backyard,

and going for nice long walks in the
neighborhood park.

Everything was perfect until Big Bob would say, "Amy, let's go for a motorcycle ride." Suddenly Little Mike and Maddie's tails would stop wagging and they didn't feel so happy anymore.

Out came a shiny red motorcycle from the garage while Amy put Little Mike and Maddie into the backyard. "We'll be home soon, my sweet peas," Amy said with a pat and a smile. "Go play with your toys."

Little Mike and Maddie didn't want to play with their toys. They wanted to go for a motorcycle ride, too, but there was only room for Big Bob and Amy. Little Mike and Maddie could only stare sadly through the fence as Big Bob and Amy rode away with a "Vrumm, vrumm!"

Maddie plopped down and put her head between her paws and Little Mike curled up beside her. Usually they took a nap until Big Bob and Amy came home, but this time they couldn't sleep. They tried lying down this way and that way and it was just no use.

Little Mike looked at Maddie, and Maddie looked at Little Mike. How they wished they were with Big Bob and Amy on the motorcycle right now! They could only imagine what it must be like to hear the wind whistling past them and see the open road in front of them. There had to be something they could do to make their dream come true.

A rustling sound made Little Mike and Maddie jump up and turn around. The wind had blown a paper bag into the backyard and it was caught in the fence. Suddenly Little Mike and Maddie got a terrific idea.

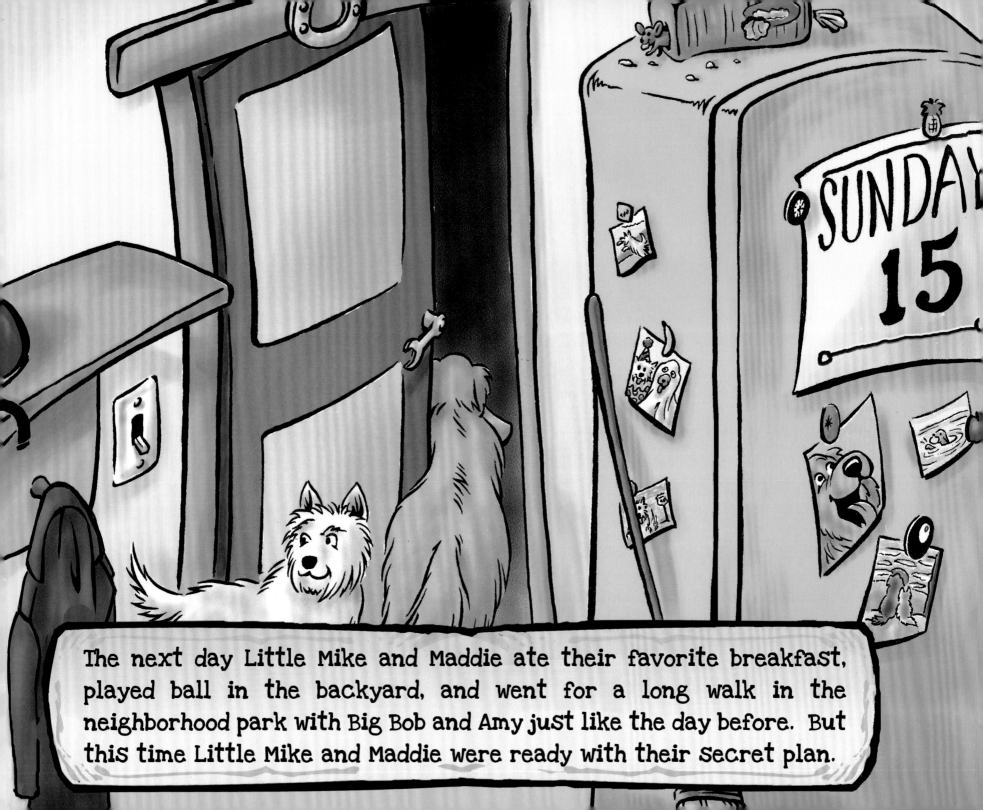

The next day Little Mike and Maddie ate their favorite breakfast, played ball in the backyard, and went for a long walk in the neighborhood park with Big Bob and Amy just like the day before. But this time Little Mike and Maddie were ready with their secret plan.

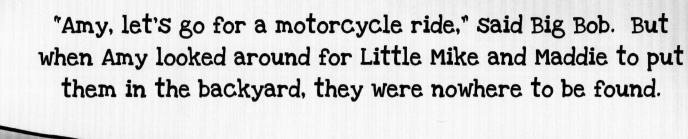

"Amy, let's go for a motorcycle ride," said Big Bob. But when Amy looked around for Little Mike and Maddie to put them in the backyard, they were nowhere to be found.

Big Bob and Amy looked upstairs and downstairs. There was still no sign of Little Mike and Maddie. Everything was way too quiet. All of their favorite toys were gone, too, like Maddie's green ball and Little Mike's squeaky yellow duck.

"Don't worry, Amy, we'll find our two fuzz balls," said Big Bob. He gave Amy a hug because he knew how much she loved the dogs. He loved them, too. Little Mike and Maddie were part of their family.

There was only one more place to look. To Big Bob's surprise, the kitchen door to the garage was open and he switched on the light.

"I've found them!" said Big Bob. He and Amy stared in amazement at Little Mike and Maddie, who had jumped onto the shiny red motorcycle and sat wagging their tails. Maddie held a paper bag in her mouth that was filled with treats and their favorite toys.

Big Bob laughed. Amy happily hugged Little Mike and Maddie. "I think Booger and Dog Breath want to go for a ride," Big Bob said to Amy with a wink. "I've got an idea. I'll be back soon."

While Big Bob was gone, Little Mike and Maddie played in the backyard with Amy. They were so busy having fun, it didn't seem like any time at all had passed before they heard the motorcycle rumbling up to the house.

Little Mike and Maddie bumped into each other in their hurry to get to the fence. Something was different. They stared at the shiny red motorcycle in surprise. It looked like it had gotten bigger! The next thing they knew, Amy called for them to come into the house.

Little Mike and Maddie followed Amy into the garage, their tails wagging with excitement. "Look, we've got room for four now," said Big Bob, waving to the shiny new red sidecar. "Jump in!"

Maddie jumped into the sidecar first and sat down. Little Mike scrambled in after a couple of hops and sat down in front of Maddie. Big Bob and Amy climbed onto the motorcycle and, "Vrumm, vrumm!" They all rode together out of the garage.

"Look at us!" barked Little Mike and Maddie to the neighbor dogs that ran to the fence to see them pass by. "Our dream has come true! It's our first motorcycle ride!"

Out on the road, Big Bob made the motorcycle go faster. Little Mike and Maddie wagged their tails as they roared past a lake where some kids were swimming. "Look at the two dogs in the sidecar!" a little boy shouted to his friends, and they all waved.

Little Mike and Maddie had never been happier. They had ridden in a car before, but on the motorcycle everything looked different. They loved the sunshine on their faces. They loved the wind blowing their ears. They loved the big blue sky above them and the open road in front of them. It was just how they imagined it would be. "It's our first motorcycle ride!" Little Mike barked to the horses in the pasture.

Big Bob and Amy looked happy, too, as they all rode together up and down the hills on the winding twisty roads. Every time another motorcycle passed by, Big Bob and Amy waved and Little Mike and Maddie barked, "Hello!"

All too soon the motorcycle ride was over. As Big Bob pulled into the driveway, Little Mike and Maddie knew they couldn't wait until the next time they zoomed down the road in the sidecar. Their fur was all rumpled, but that was part of the fun. It had been the most wonderful day!

After supper, Little Mike and Maddie snuggled into their cozy dog bed. They couldn't wait to fall asleep and dream about the places they would go with Big Bob and Amy and the fun things they would do. Little Mike nudged Maddie with his nose. "Good night, Maddie May." Maddie curled up closer to Little Mike. "Good night, Mikey."

Little Mike and Maddie closed their eyes and dreamed of a shiny red sidecar and the wind in their ears and the big blue sky above them and all the exciting motorcycle adventures to come. Vrumm, vrumm . . .